George's Marvellous Medicine

LEVEL 5

Re-told by: Andy Hopkins
Series Editor: Melanie Williams

Pearson Education Limited
Edinburgh Gate, Harlow,
Essex CM20 2JE, England
and Associated Companies throughout the world.

ISBN: 978-1-4082-8836-8

This edition first published by Pearson Education Ltd 2014

1 3 5 7 9 10 8 6 4 2

Text copyright © Pearson Education Ltd 2014

Copyright © Roald Dahl Nominee Ltd 2014

Illustrations copyright © Quentin Blake, 1981
Set in 15/19pt OT Fiendstar
Printed in China
SWTC/01
Published by Pearson Education Ltd in association with
Penguin Books Ltd, a Penguin Random House company.

For a complete list of the titles available in the Penguin Kids series please go to www.penguinreaders.com.
Alternatively, write to your local Pearson Education office or to: Penguin Readers Marketing Department,
Pearson Education, Edinburgh Gate, Harlow, Essex CM20 2JE, England.

'I'm going shopping,' George's mother said. 'Be a good boy. And don't forget to give your grandmother her medicine at eleven o'clock!'

Eight-year-old George Kranky was bored. He lived on a farm a long way from the village, so there were no other children to play with. He had no brothers or sisters. And he did not like living with his grandmother. Most grandmothers are kind and loving, but not this one. She was a selfish, grumpy old woman.

Grandma sat in her chair all day. She never smiled or said anything nice. She frightened George. And she was *really* nasty when his parents were out.

'Come here and I'll tell you secrets,' she said with a cold smile. 'Don't be afraid of your old grandmother.' She laughed. 'I have magic powers. I can change the shapes of animals — and little children too.'

George wanted to run away, but he could not move. Was his grandmother a witch?

'I can change *your* shape,' Grandma said, 'or I can make teeth grow out of your fingers.' George's eyes grew wider. His grandmother's eyes were ice cold. 'Or I can give you a long tail ...'

'Grandma!' George cried. 'Stop!'

But she did not stop. 'I know secrets about dark places where dark things live ...'

George ran for the door.

'You can't get away,' she shouted after him.

George ran into the kitchen and shut the door quickly behind him.

CHAPTER 2

George *hated* his grandmother.

'I'm not afraid of her,' he thought angrily.

But he was.

'What can I do to frighten *her*?' he thought. 'Perhaps I can put a snake down her dress! Or I can put six mice in her room and shut the door!'

But he did not have a snake or any mice. Then he saw the bottle of Grandma's brown medicine on the kitchen table and, suddenly, he had a marvellous idea!

'I'll make her a magic medicine!' George thought. 'I'll make it very strong. Perhaps then she'll become a better person ... or her head will explode!'

It was five past ten, nearly an hour until the time for Grandma's medicine.

'I'll start now,' he thought. He began to sing –

'Will she pop? Will she explode?
Will she go flying down the road?
Who knows? Not me. Let's wait and see.
I'm happy it's not you or me.

CHAPTER 3

George took a large pot out of the cupboard and put it on the table. He decided to make the medicine from all the runny, powdery or gooey things in the house.

First, he went to the bathroom. He put in a big bottle of shampoo and some face cream. Then he found some yellow hair oil. That went in too. Bottles of this and bottles of that — everything went into George's big pot.

In the kitchen, George put in a whole box of washing powder —
and some brown shoe polish too, because Grandma's medicine
was brown. Then he looked in the food cupboards. There were
a lot of bottles, bags and boxes in different colours. What was
in them? He did not know. But it all went in!

'George!' Grandma shouted. 'Is it time for my medicine?'

'In about half an hour, Grandma,' he answered.

'Don't forget!'

'I won't, Grandma,' George answered.

Then George had another good idea. 'I'll look in the small barn next to the chicken house,' he thought. 'All the animal medicines are in there!'

He picked up the heavy pot and went out. In the barn, he found five bottles. There were horse pills, a powder for chickens and some gooey stuff for cows and sheep. He put them all in.

'Fantastic,' he thought. 'I'll give that grumpy Grandma a big drink of this!'

George stirred his marvellous medicine. It was thick and gooey and full of beautiful colours – pinks, blues, greens, yellows and browns. But you could still see the pills.

'I'll have to cook it,' he thought.

On the way back to the house, he saw some car oil and brown paint in the garage. He put them in his pot. Then he went to the kitchen and started cooking.

'Where's my medicine?' his Grandma shouted.

'Not long now, Grandma,' he called.

The stuff in the pot got hotter and hotter. George stirred the gooey medicine again. The kitchen was full of thick blue smoke, and there was a terrible smell.

Now George was excited. His eyes opened wide and strange words came into his head from nowhere. Suddenly he began to dance round the kitchen and sing. He sang a song about his magic medicine.

CHAPTER 4

'Open your mouth wide, Grandma,' said George.

The old woman opened her small mouth and showed her ugly brown teeth. George pushed the spoon in – and waited.

'OWEEE!' shouted Grandma, and shot up into the air.

Her eyes were wide and her hair stood up straight. Her body did not move. It just sat there, high above George.

'Is something wrong, Grandma?' he asked kindly.

Suddenly – **PLOP** – Grandma fell back down into her chair.

'My stomach's on fire!' Grandma shouted. Black smoke poured out of her mouth.

George ran for water and threw it into her mouth. But then her body began to get bigger. Her face became purple, then green.

'She's going to explode!' thought George. 'How interesting!'

But she started to get smaller again. Then a funny thing happened. Grandma jumped out of her chair and stood up without her stick.

'Marvellous medicine,' thought George. 'What next?'

He soon found out.

Grandma started to grow. She grew taller and taller.

George could not believe his eyes. She went up and up, through the ceiling, into his bedroom. He ran upstairs.

'Here I come,' shouted Grandma. At last, she could speak. 'This medicine's fantastic! Give me more!'

George gave her some more and she grew again. She went through the ceiling of George's bedroom and up towards the roof!

'Not the roof!' thought George. 'Dad is going to be so angry!'

CHAPTER 5

Grandma's head and shoulders broke out through the roof.

'I feel fantastic! You see, I *have* got magic powers!'

'But Grandma, *I* made this medicine,' shouted George.

'I don't believe you,' she shouted back.

'Watch this, then.'

George poured some medicine onto a spoon and walked towards a chicken. Like Grandma, the chicken shot into the air, then came down. After that, smoke poured from its mouth. George threw water over it. Then the chicken started to grow.

'Look!' George shouted. 'I gave it the magic medicine and it's growing, just like you.'

The chicken got bigger and bigger, but it also got fatter and fatter. When it stopped, it was the size of a horse.

'It's not as tall as me,' shouted Grandma. 'I'm the tallest!'

Then George's mother came back from the shops. She saw the enormous chicken. She saw Grandma's head above the roof. 'What's happening?' she asked. She could not believe her eyes!

'It's George's medicine!' shouted Grandma. 'He gave it to me and the chicken.'

Just then, George's father arrived. Mr Kranky looked at the chicken. 'What's this? How did this happen?' he asked. 'It's enormous!'

'I did it,' George said. He started to tell his father about the magic medicine. Suddenly, the chicken sat down and went *cluck*. They all looked at it. When it stood up again, there was a brown egg. It was the size of a football.

Mr Kranky was very excited.

'How much of this medicine have you got?' he asked.

'A lot,' said George.

'Come with me,' his father said. 'Let's try it on the other animals.'

They gave the magic medicine to the cows, the sheep and the horses. And the same thing happened with each of the animals. First, there was a lot of smoke. Then the animals ran and jumped. Then they grew and grew and grew!

'Hey!' Grandma called from the roof. 'I want a cup of tea!'

'Don't listen to her,' Mr Kranky laughed. 'Let's leave her there.'

'We can't! She's my mother,' said Mrs Kranky.

In the end, they phoned for a crane to pull her out.

The medicine did not make Grandma nicer, but she felt young again. She rode one of the big horses round the farm. Then she slept in the big barn because she was too tall for the house.

CHAPTER 6

'We must make more of your magic medicine,' George's father said the next morning.

'Why?' George asked. 'All our animals are bigger now.'

'Because every farmer wants enormous animals!' he said. 'We can make a lot of money, and there will be no hungry people in the world!'

'But Dad ...' said George, 'I put hundreds of things in the pot. I can't remember them all.'

'Yes, you can,' said his father. 'I'll help you.'

They went to the bathroom and the kitchen. They went to the barn and the garage. George tried hard to remember everything. His father wrote it down.

Then Mr Kranky drove his car to the village. He bought new shampoos, creams, oils and powders. He bought more pills, and a lot of gooey stuff for animals. Then he took it all back to George.

'Now, how did you make the medicine?' he asked his son.

CHAPTER 7

'What did you put in first?' asked Mr Kranky.

'This,' said George, and he picked up some shampoo.
'Then some of this cream, I think. And some of this hair oil.'

He opened the bottles and poured them into the pot.

'That's it, my boy! Don't stop!' his father said.

George put more runny, powdery and gooey things in the pot.

'Then what did you do?' Mr Kranky asked. 'Did you stir it?'

'Yes. And it has to be hot,' George said.

He made it hot and stirred it well.

'You mustn't forget anything,' said his father, 'or the medicine won't work.'

George thought hard. 'We haven't got any brown paint!'

Mr Kranky drove to the village and came back with some paint.

George stirred it in. 'That's better,' he said. 'It's the right colour now too.'

At last, it was ready.

Mr Kranky was excited. 'Let's give some to a chicken!'

George gave Marvellous Medicine Number Two to a black-and-white chicken.

whoosh!

The chicken shot up into the air and came down again. Then fire – not smoke – came from its mouth, and its legs grew longer. Its body stayed the same size, but its two thin yellow legs got longer and longer and longer ...

'It's not right!' cried Mr Kranky. 'You forgot something.'
George thought. 'Shoe polish! I forgot the shoe polish.'
Mr Kranky ran to his car.

'Here it is,' said George's father. 'Brown shoe polish.'

George put the polish in the pot and stirred it well. Then they gave Marvellous Medicine Number Three to a black chicken.

Again, the chicken shot up in the air and came back down.

'Now watch!' Mr Kranky cried.

The chicken did not move at first. Then, suddenly, its neck started to grow!

'You can't eat a chicken's neck!' Mrs Kranky said.

But the neck grew longer and longer.

'I know,' George said. 'Last time, I put some car oil in.'

'That's the answer!' Mr Kranky cried.

George poured Marvellous Medicine Number Four into a cup and gave some to a brown chicken.

This time, it did not shoot up in the air.

'It's not moving,' said Mrs Kranky.

They looked carefully at the brown chicken.

'It's getting smaller,' George said.

And in less than a minute, the chicken was smaller than an egg. It looked very silly.

CHAPTER 8

'You'll never get it right,' Mrs Kranky said sadly.

Just then, Grandma came outside. She was still very tall.

'Where's my tea?' she asked. She saw the cup in George's hand. 'I'll have *that*,' she said.

'But Grandma ...' George said.

'Give it to me NOW.'

'No, Mother ...' said Mrs Kranky.

'I want that tea, NOW,' Grandma shouted.

Mr Kranky smiled up at the nasty old woman. 'OK, Grandma. Drink it now. It's nice and hot.'

She took the cup and drank quickly. A strange noise came from her mouth.

'This is going to be interesting,' Mr Kranky said.

'You did this!' Mrs Kranky shouted at her husband. 'She's going to explode!'

But suddenly, Grandma started to get smaller.

Soon she was her usual size. Then she was the size of a cat ... then a mouse ... then a fly ...

'Where is she?' cried Mrs Kranky. 'She's not here!'

'HOORAY'! said Mr Kranky.

'Bad things happen to nasty people,' said Mr Kranky.

For a few minutes, Mrs Kranky looked for her mother. 'Where are you?' she called. 'How can I find you?'

But she soon stopped looking.

'Perhaps it's better this way,' she said. 'She *was* a grumpy, selfish old woman.'

'Yes, she was,' Mr Kranky agreed.

George did not speak, but he learned something new that day. For a very short time, he saw – and touched – a magic world.

Before You Read

**❶ Look at the picture.
What do you think?**
  a What is the boy's name?
  b Where is he?
  c What is he making?

**❷ Do these words describe a person who you like? Or do
they describe a person who you don't like? You can use
your dictionary.**

> nasty   nice   selfish   kind   grumpy
> marvellous   fantastic   terrible   boring   interesting

❸ Match the words to the pictures. You can use a dictionary.

> face cream   oil   pills   powder   polish   shampoo

ⓐ   ⓒ   ⓔ

ⓑ   ⓓ   ⓕ

Activity page ②

After You Read

1 **What happened the first time George gave Grandma his medicine? Put the sentences in the right order.**

a She grew taller and taller.

b Her body grew smaller.

c Her body grew bigger and bigger.

d Smoke poured out of her mouth.

e She shot up into the air.

f She became purple and then green.

2 **Finish these sentences.**

a George and Mr Kranky gave the medicine to _____.
   1 the chickens **2** the cows, sheep and horses **3** Mrs Kranky

b With Marvellous Medicine Number Two, the chicken grew _____.
   1 very long legs   **2** a very fat body   **3** a very big head

c With Marvellous Medicine Number Three, the chicken grew _____
   1 very large wings   **2** very big feet   **3** a very long neck

d George added _____ to make Marvellous Medicine Number Four.
   1 car oil   **2** polish   **3** paint

3 **What happened to Grandma in the end? How did her family feel about this? Why?**